Borgon the Axeboy

AND THE WHISPERING TEMPLE

ABOUT THE AUTHOR

KJARTAN POSKITT is the well-loved author of many hilarious books for children including Agatha Parrot and the Murderous Maths series, translated into over 30 languages. With a background in children's television, he is a tireless and brilliant performer.

ABOUT THE ILLUSTRATOR

PHILIP REEVE is an award-winning illustrator and author whose books have won the Carnegie, Guardian and Smarties Prizes.

Borgon the Axeboy

AND THE WHISPERING TEMPLE

Kjartan Poskitt

Illustrated by

Philip Reeve

ff

FABER & FABER

First published in 2015
by Faber & Faber Limited
Bloomsbury House
74–77 Great Russell Street
London WC1B 3DA

Designed by Faber
Printed and bound by CPI Group (UK) Ltd, Croydon CR4 0YY

A CIP record for this book is available from the British Library

978–0–571–30737–1

2 4 6 8 10 9 7 5 3 1

To Joshua Burland

GRUMBLE
GRUMBLE

GOLGARTH BASIN
THE FIRE LANDS
RARGH!
HERE BE DRAGONS
THE PUNCH PIT
THE UPSIDE-DOWN MOUNTAINS
THE LOST DESERT

MOUNTAINS OF CHAOS
BOO-BA-DE-DOO
WAH OOOH
SHABBADA BE-BOO-BA DOOP
YEAH!
VALLEY OF THE SCAT CACTI
THE WANDERING JUNGLE
CONFUSED BUSH
N
THE LOST DESSERT
RUINED TEMPLE

The Blue Snake

It was morning in the Lost Desert. The
sunlight was shining on the ruins of an old
temple hidden among the giant rocks, and
a bright blue rattlesnake was quietly dozing
high up on a window ledge. Suddenly . . .

PLOP!

A fat raindrop splatted down on to the

snake's head. The snake opened a beady eye and saw a huge black cloud shutting out the sun. The snake knew the raindrop hadn't been an accident. Softly, it uncoiled itself, then listened out very carefully. Sure enough, there was the sound of something climbing up from below. The snake opened its mouth wide so its fangs were ready to strike, then it peered over the edge to see who or what was coming.

'GOTCHA!'

A dirty hand grabbed the snake by the neck and dragged it off the ledge. The snake thrashed around helplessly in the air, then realised it was being stared in the face by

a chubby little savage. The snake tried to
stretch forward and sink its fangs into his
nose, but the savage just laughed.

'You ARE a beauty!' said Borgon the
Axeboy.

HISS! SPIT! Rattle rattle! went
the snake angrily.

'Behave yourself,' laughed Borgon.

He scrambled back down the wall,
holding the snake out at arm's length.

Three more savages were waiting at the bottom. Grizzy was the girl with the shoulder bag, Mungoid was the chunky one and Hunjah was the skinny one with the big straw hat. All four of them lived in a circle of caves known as Golgarth Basin, and that morning they had been exploring when Borgon had spotted the snake.

Of course, any sensible savage would have kept well away from the snake, but Borgon was not a sensible savage. He was a barbarian, which meant he was one of the fiercest, scariest and maddest savages in the desert. For Borgon there was no such thing as fear, there was only fun, and that's why catching rattlesnakes was one of his favourite tricks.

'Look at this!' said Borgon, as he jumped to the ground. 'I'm going to keep it for a pet.'

'Put it back!' said Hunjah nervously.

'Not likely,' said Borgon. 'I've never seen a blue rattlesnake before.'

'Me neither,' said Mungoid. 'Rattlers are

supposed to be yellow or brown so they can hide in the rocks.'

'That's not a normal rattlesnake,' said Hunjah nervously. 'It's a guard snake.'

'Rubbish,' said Grizzy. 'Whoever heard of a guard snake? What's it supposed to be guarding?'

'The temple!' said Hunjah. 'I've just recognised it. My mum used to be a priestess here. She took me inside once when I was small and she warned me about the blue snakes.'

'So what happened to this place?' asked Mungoid, looking up at the ruins. 'Doesn't anybody come here any more?'

'Not since the earthquake,' said Hunjah.

'EARTHQUAKE?' gasped the others.

'Did the land split open and mountains collapse?' asked Mungoid.

'Not really,' said Hunjah sadly. 'But the temple wobbled a bit and some big stones fell off, so everybody decided it was unsafe and stopped coming.'

'Not everybody!' said Borgon, holding up the snake. 'This guy's still here.'

'You'd better let the snake go,' said Hunjah. 'Or you'll upset the temple god.'

'Who cares?' said Borgon. 'I'm a BARBARIAN! If there is a god still in there, he should be more worried about upsetting me. **YARGHHHH!**'

7

KABLOOSH!

A blast of rain came down and sploshed Borgon from head to toe. The hot sand around his feet fizzed and gave off a cloud of steam.

'HA HA HA!' laughed Grizzy.

'It's not funny,' said Hunjah. 'That was the god sending Borgon a warning.'

'Don't be so pathetic, Hunjah,' said Grizzy. 'This temple is a wreck. No sensible god would still be hanging around when there's no one coming to worship him.'

'Are you sure?' asked Mungoid, looking uncertain. 'It's funny how that bit of rain just hit Borgon and nothing else.'

Borgon looked at the ground. There was

only one wet patch
and he was standing
in the middle of it. The
snake gave its tail a little
waggle. It seemed to be
laughing at him.

'If there is a god
here wanting to scare
me, he'll have to try
harder than that!' said
Borgon.

Above them the dark
cloud rumbled. Mungoid looked up nervously.

'Maybe you shouldn't have said that,' said
the chunky savage.

9

'Drop the snake,' said Hunjah. 'Or the god will make it worse.'

'Oh really?' said Borgon. 'So what's he going to do then?'

More rain started coming down, and this time it was hitting all of them.

'Told you!' said Hunjah.

'Oh, be quiet, you three,' said Grizzy. 'There's no god around here!'

'There might be,' said Mungoid nervously.

'There IS!' insisted Hunjah.

'No there is NOT!' said Grizzy. 'It's just rain and I'm getting wet, so let's go.'

The four of them dashed round the outside of the temple looking for cover, then

Borgon fell over and landed flat on his face.

BLOMP!

The snake slipped out of his hand then whipped round to strike at him. Borgon just managed to roll aside, and snatch the creature up by the neck again.

'You were lucky there,' said Hunjah. 'The god tripped you up on purpose.'

'No he didn't,' said Borgon.

'Hunjah's right!' said Mungoid. 'There's a giant foot sticking out of the sand!'

'That's not a god's foot,' said Grizzy looking around. 'It's just part of a statue. There's broken bits of arms and legs lying all over the place.'

Sure enough, there was.

'I remember that statue,' said Hunjah. 'It was a giant soldier, and he used to stand outside the temple door. Look!'

Hunjah was pointing at a small archway in the temple wall, which was completely sealed off by a flat slab of stone. The rain was coming down even harder.

'How does it open, Hunjah?' asked Grizzy. 'Quick, I'm soaking.'

'The stone slides

upwards,' said Hunjah. 'But it can only be lifted by the god himself.'

'Then tell him to get on with it, if you're so sure he's here,' said Grizzy.

Meanwhile Borgon and Mungoid were admiring the snake.

'Look at those fangs!' said Borgon. 'This fella could bring down an elephant.'

'Then you'd better let him go!' said Mungoid.

'You worry too much,' laughed Borgon.

'But what if Hunjah's god is real?' said Mungoid. 'Some of these old desert gods can do strange and terrible things. He might turn the snake into a giant serpent and swallow you up!'

'Then I'll be ready for it!' said Borgon, waving his axe excitedly. '**YARGHHH!**'

Hunjah was tapping on the temple door politely.

'Hello? Excuse me? Yoo-hoo!'

Nothing happened.

Grizzy pointed at a small dark hole drilled high into the side of the arch. Around it was carved an image of the sun.

'What's that for?' she asked.

'I don't know,' said Hunjah. 'Maybe we have to talk into it.'

'Let me try,' said Grizzy. 'Hey, Mungoid, help me up!'

16

The chunky
savage went to
stand by the arch,
then Grizzy climbed
up and stood on his
head. She shouted
into the hole. 'HEY
YOU! If you ARE a
god in there, OPEN
UP!'

Still nothing
happened, and
the rain was still
falling.

'Oh, what

a surprise,' said Grizzy. She jumped down to the ground. 'There's no god, and I'm soaking. Come on, you lot, there must be somewhere we can shelter.'

The temple was built into the side of a small cliff. Halfway up, a withered old cactus was growing near the entrance to a small tunnel. They scrambled up the rocks and ducked inside, then stood there shivering, looking out at the water hitting the hot rocks and hissing up into little puffs of steam.

'This is all your fault, Borgon!' said Hunjah.

'Let the snake go, and then the god might forgive you.'

'For the last time, there isn't a god!' said Grizzy.

'That's not fair,' said Borgon. 'There might be a god, but maybe he's just a bit pathetic, like Hunjah is.'

'Thanks, Borgon!' said Hunjah happily. 'See, Grizzy? Borgon believes me.'

'So what's this god of yours called then?' asked Grizzy.

'His followers know him as . . .'

Hunjah paused, then put on his deepest and most serious voice.

'. . . the Great Conk.'

'The Great Conk?' repeated the others. 'Ha ha ha ha ha!'

KAKKA-KABOOSH!

A lightning bolt hit the old cactus, which burst into flames.

'Ooh!' said Hunjah. 'I didn't know he could do that.'

Can Water Fly?

Borgon, Mungoid, Grizzy and Hunjah were
still sitting in the tunnel entrance waiting for
the rain to stop. A little stream of water was
coming down the side of the cliff, running
past their feet and disappearing down into
the darkness of the tunnel. Borgon was
holding the snake and stroking its head.

The poor beast had given up wriggling and was now just looking very fed up.

'This is getting boring,' said Grizzy.

'Then let the snake go!' said Hunjah.

'Why?' asked Borgon. 'It's just a snake.'

'No it is NOT!' insisted Hunjah. 'It is a servant of the Great Conk.'

'I'm fed up of hearing about this stupid god of yours,' said Grizzy. 'There's no such thing as the Great Conk.'

'Oh really?' said Hunjah. 'Then where do you think this rain is coming from? I'll tell you – he's sending it down out of his big nose!'

'His BIG NOSE?' said the other three. They all looked out of the tunnel entrance.

'I can't see a big nose,' said Grizzy. 'Just a
dirty black cloud.'

'It is a bit nose-shaped though,' said
Mungoid.

'So it is!' agreed Borgon.

'So what?' snapped Grizzy. 'Rain does
NOT come out of a god's nose. It's all
explained in here.'

She pulled a thick book from her bag. It
was called the *Book of All Things* and it knew
everything about everything, and even a
little bit more. Grizzy flicked through the
pages.

'Aha! Found it!' she said. 'How rain is
made . . . the sun heats up water in lakes and

23

it rises up into the air.'

'You mean the sun makes the water fly?' gasped Mungoid.

'I suppose so,' said Grizzy. 'Then the water turns into a cloud, and then the cloud flies over us and the water falls down again.'

'Ha ha ha!' laughed the boys.

'You mean to say that big cloud up there is a load of flying water?' said Mungoid.

'But water is heavy!' said Hunjah. 'Why doesn't it all just fall down at once with a big **SPLOSH**?'

'Hunjah's got a point,' said Borgon. 'What do you think, Mungoid? Is that a cloud of flying water, or is it a god's nose?'

'Water can't fly,' said Mungoid. 'So Hunjah must be right. That cloud MUST be the Great Conk's nose!'

'No it is NOT!' said Grizzy crossly.

'There's one way to find out,' said Hunjah. 'Borgon lets the snake go, and we see if the rain stops.'

'Of course it won't stop,' said Grizzy.

But Hunjah stuck his head out of the cave and shouted up at the cloud.

'Oh, Great Conk! Please stop the rain when Borgon lets the snake go!'

'Hang on!' said Borgon. 'I never agreed to let it go.'

'But you have to!' said Hunjah. 'Or Grizzy won't believe me.'

'Too right I won't believe you,' giggled Grizzy.

'Please, Borgon,' said Hunjah. 'Please?'

Borgon sighed. Hunjah was looking really upset, and there was only one way to settle the argument. Borgon held up the snake so he could speak to it face to face.

'Are you going to behave?' he asked.

The snake just stuck out its tongue rudely.

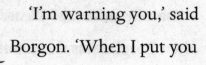

'I'm warning you,' said Borgon. 'When I put you

down, if you try to be clever, I'll slice you into bootlaces.'

The others all backed away as far as they could.

'You're not letting it go in here?' asked Grizzy.

'He'll be fine,' said Borgon.

He put the snake on the ground then released its neck. The snake snapped at Borgon's hand, but it wasn't fast enough. The axeboy slapped the side of its head.

'I'm warning you,' he said. 'Bootlaces!'

The snake slithered away, following the stream of water down into the darkness of the tunnel, shaking its tail as it went . . .

Rattle rattle rattle ...

The rattling tail got quieter and quieter, and as it did so the rain stopped and the sun came out.

'Told you, Grizzy!' said Hunjah, with a happy little smile.

Grizzy slammed her book shut. 'That was just luck,' she snapped.

Suddenly, a much louder sound came booming out of the darkness:

RATTLE RATTLE RATTLE!

'What's that?' asked Hunjah.

'I'm going to find out!' said Borgon.

'Watch out, Borgon,' said Mungoid.

'Maybe the Great Conk HAS turned the snake into a giant serpent.'

Borgon pulled out his axe and grinned. 'Then I'll be making a lot of bootlaces!'

The Lucky Hat

Borgon followed the little stream of water down into the dark tunnel. The path got narrower and narrower and darker and darker, it twisted and turned and soon everything was too black to see. Ahead he could hear the snake waiting for him.

RATTLE rattle HISSS! RATTLE

HISS! Rattle RATTLE!

Borgon's shoulders were bruised from scraping along the walls, his feet were soaking from stepping in the water, his face was covered in old sticky cobwebs, and he was on his way to fight a giant serpent in the dark.

'**YARGHHH!**' shouted Borgon happily.

Some days being a barbarian was just such good fun.

Finally he came to a dead end. Borgon felt around the walls and realised he was standing in a small chamber. The rattle noise stopped and the last echoes faded away to silence. Borgon couldn't see a thing, but the barbarian wasn't worried. He held his breath and listened, with his axe ready to strike at the first sound of movement.

'Where are you?' he whispered. 'Come on!'

Borgon walked around, scuffing the ground with his feet to see if he could find the snake. Suddenly . . .

'WAAAAA . . . !'

Borgon yelped in surprise as his legs fell through two holes in the floor and his bottom hit the ground with a solid BUMP. It was like wearing a big pair of solid stone pants. He could feel his feet dangling in empty space and, worst of all, the water from the tunnel was pouring into the top of his trousers, running down his legs and out past his boots.

'. . . **AHHHHH!**'

Borgon's cry was still echoing around, even though he'd stopped shouting. There was a flicker in the darkness.

'There he is!' said Mungoid's voice.

The chunky savage was making his way down the tunnel holding a burning branch from the old cactus and leading the other two.

'Oh no!' said Hunjah. 'Borgon's been bitten in half by the giant serpent!'

'Sadly not,' said Grizzy.

'There's no giant serpent,' said Borgon.

'There's just a giant ECHO!'

Echo echo echo . . .

As Mungoid brought the flame closer,
Borgon could see that the wall had two more
holes that were side by side like little windows.

Mungoid and Hunjah took Borgon's arms and heaved him up on to his feet. They looked down the floor holes, but all they could see was the water dripping away and falling into darkness.

Mungoid shouted out through one of the holes in the wall.

'Hell-oo!'

HELL-OOOO! the echo boomed back loud and low, making all their teeth shake.

'Wow!' said Mungoid. 'The blue snake must have crawled in there, and that's why the rattles are so loud.'

'I want a go!' said Hunjah.

He stuck his head out of one of the holes

and shouted . . .

'Hell . . . oh no!'

HELL . . . OH NOOOOOOO! came

the echo.

Hunjah pulled his head back.

'Where's your hat gone?' asked Grizzy.

'It fell off!' said Hunjah, panicking. 'My

mum will go mad. I need to wear it all the

time to stop the sun cooking my brain.'

'It's down there,' said Mungoid, looking

through one of the floor holes. 'You're lucky,

I think it's caught on something.'

'I'll try to reach it,' said Hunjah. He stuck

his hand down the hole.

Rattle rattle rattle!

'Oh no!' said Hunjah, pulling his hand back sharply. 'The snake's down there. I'll never get it now.'

'Let me do it,' said Borgon. He took Hunjah's place and stuck his arm down into the darkness.

Rattle rattle rattle!

Borgon felt the faintest movement of air on the back of his hand as the snake struck, but once again the barbarian was too fast. He pushed the creature out of the way, grabbed the hat and pulled it up.

'There you go, Hunjah,' said Borgon.

'Thanks!' said Hunjah. He was just about to put it on his head when something fell out.

'It's a gold coin,' said Borgon.

'Then you better keep it,' said Hunjah. 'After all, you found it.'

'I wonder if there are any more down there?' said Grizzy.

She took the burning branch from Mungoid then stuck it down through the hole as far as she could. Two beady eyes glinted back at her.

Rattle rattle rattle!

Suddenly the flame flared up Grizzy's arm.

'Ouch!' she yelped and dropped the branch. The flame fell and exploded in a shower of sparks, then splashed into a puddle of water far below them. Everything went black, but not before they'd seen a flash of what was down there.

'It's like a huge room,' said Mungoid. 'With strange shapes on the walls!'

'And I saw something else,' said Grizzy.

'What?' asked the others.

'The other side of the arch,' said Grizzy. 'This tunnel we've just come down must be a secret back way into the temple.'

'Then I know exactly where we are!' said Hunjah excitedly. 'We are inside the nose of the Great Conk.'

'What?' snapped Grizzy.

'If you walk in through the temple door, you can see a giant head of the Conk at the far end,' said Hunjah. 'But this tunnel has brought us into the back of the head. These two holes in the wall are the eyeholes and . . .'

'Don't tell me,' snapped Grizzy. 'These holes in the floor are the nose holes.'

'Oh!' said Borgon. 'That's why his nose drips! It's from this little stream coming down the tunnel.'

'So you mean to say
I'm standing in the
dark inside a giant
dripping nose?'
asked
Grizzy.

'Yes!' said Hunjah excitedly.

'Oh gross!' said Grizzy.

Who Nibbled A Whole Hippopotamus?

It had been a long morning, and exploring tunnels was hungry work. By the time Borgon got home to Golgarth Basin, he was glad to see his dad was getting lunch ready. Fulgut was a huge old barbarian, and there was only one thing he liked more than

lunch. It was more lunch. He was chopping up a big wobbly hippopotamus liver.

'Is that all we've got, Dad?' said Borgon. 'I'm starving.'

'Don't moan,' said Fulgut. 'You like hippo liver.'

'I know, but where's the rest of the hippo?'

asked Borgon. 'We only caught it yesterday.'

'Ah, well, er . . .' said Fulgut, looking sheepish. 'I had a little nibble at it this morning.'

'What?' said Borgon. 'Do you mean to say you nibbled away a WHOLE HIPPOPOTAMUS?'

Just then Borgon's mum came through from the back of the cave. Fulma was tall with spiky hair and long pin-pointed teeth.

'How's that hippopotamus coming along?' she asked.

'We've only got the liver,' said Borgon. 'Dad ate the rest.'

'Oh, not AGAIN!' Fulma hissed angrily.

Her hair stuck out and her eyes narrowed. No wonder she was known as the scariest savage in the Lost Desert!

'Don't you want this liver?' asked Fulgut nervously.

'No I do NOT,' said Fulma. She waved a long bony finger in Fulgut's face. 'Why would I want some SMELLY OLD LIVER that EVEN YOU couldn't be bothered to eat?'

'Please, dear, don't

be upset!' said Fulgut. 'If you like, we'll just pop out and hunt you something even better than hippo, won't we, Borgon?'

'Good idea, Dad!' said Borgon. 'How about a nice juicy giraffe, Mum? Or a big beefy bear? Or there's even some monster tortoises in the jungle with crunchy shells. They're yummy!'

'Just tell us what you want,' said Fulgut. 'We'll get anything you like.'

'Anything at all?' said Fulma. She scratched her chin with her long bony finger and had a little think. 'Well, there IS one thing I would like, but I know I won't get it.'

'Yes you will,' said Fulgut.

'And that's a promise,' said Borgon. 'Whatever it is, however big, however nasty. So what do you want, Mum?'

'Peaches.'

'Peaches?' asked Borgon. 'What are peaches?'

'They're like squishy balls with wooden bits in the middle,' said Fulma. 'The middle's nice and crunchy but the squishy bits are horrible.'

'They sound great!' said Borgon. 'Come on, Dad, let's go and hunt for peaches. I hope they're dangerous. **YARGHHHH!**'

Borgon was already on his feet with his axe ready.

'Don't get excited, son,' sighed Fulgut. 'Peaches grow on trees.'

'Trees?' said Borgon. 'How are we supposed to hunt trees?'

'You don't need to hunt anything,' said Fulma. 'They have baskets full of peaches in the market. I could buy some.'

'But you need money for the market,' said Fulgut. 'And we don't have any.'

'See?' snapped Fulma. 'I told you I wouldn't get what I want.'

'You might do, Mum!' said Borgon. 'Is this thing any good?'

He pulled the gold coin from his pocket

and passed it to his mum.

'Goodness!' exclaimed Fulma. 'It's very pretty. I'm sure that's all I'll need. Thank you!'

'Not so fast,' said Fulgut. 'Borgon, where did you get that?'

'Hunjah gave it to me for saving his hat,' said Borgon.

'Then give it back right now,' demanded Fulgut, and he banged the table with his big fist. 'We're supposed to be barbarians, the wildest savages in the desert! We go hunting. We don't go shopping like little soft people. Everyone will laugh at us.'

'So how is Mum going to get her peaches then?' asked Borgon.

'I don't know and I don't care,' said Fulgut. The old savage went and stood in the entrance of the cave so nobody could get past. He put on his biggest and toughest voice.

'Fulma, that coin will only bring us trouble. I FORBID you to spend it in the market.'

'Oh, do you?' said Fulma. 'You should have thought of that before you scoffed that hippo. So are you going to get out of my

51

way, or do I have to do this . . . ?'

She stuck her long bony finger out again and wiggled it in the air.

'No, Fulma!' begged Fulgut. 'Be reasonable. Please don't . . .'

Borgon quickly looked away. He knew what was going to happen and he couldn't bear to watch. He even tried to block his ears, but it didn't stop him hearing the screams from his father as Fulma jabbed her finger deep into Fulgut's tummy.

'Wah ha ha!' yelped Fulgut. 'No, stoppit, get OFF!'

Borgon shuddered. Even though Fulgut could stand up to the nastiest weapons or the

fiercest creatures, he was absolutely helpless
when Fulma tickled him to death.

'Ha ha ha!' shrieked the big barbarian. 'No

really, I mean it, ha ha, I SURRENDER!'

But Fulma wasn't in the mood to show mercy. She kept tickling until the mighty savage collapsed on to the floor with tears streaming down his face. Fulma stepped over him and set off out of the cave.

'Don't say I didn't warn you!' gasped Fulgut, as she went. 'Money always brings trouble. You wait and see.'

The Sun Lock

Borgon went out to help Fulma on to her horse, then waved goodbye as she galloped off to the market. Hunjah and Mungoid came over to watch her go.

'She's in a rush!' said Mungoid.

'I gave her that gold coin,' said Borgon. 'She's gone to spend it before my dad can stop her!'

Just then Grizzy came running over. She was waving her *Book of All Things*.

'Hey, you lot, look at this!' she said.

She was pointing at one of the pages. It had a picture of the sun,

with a small black hole drawn in the middle.

'It's the same sun picture that we saw by the temple door,' said Grizzy.

'So what?' said Borgon.

'The book says it's a sun lock,' said Grizzy. 'When sunlight shines into the hole, the door opens.'

'But the sun passes right over the top of the temple,' said Borgon. 'If the lock needs sunlight, it should have been facing upwards. It'll never get any light where it is.'

'It's a bit of a mystery,' said Mungoid.

'Hey, Hunjah,' said Grizzy. 'Why did the clots who built your temple put a sun lock in the wrong place?'

'I don't know,' said Hunjah, peering into Grizzy's book. 'But that's what the statue outside used to look like.'

Hunjah was pointing at the next page.

There was
a picture of
an old soldier
holding a shield
in the air at
arm's length.

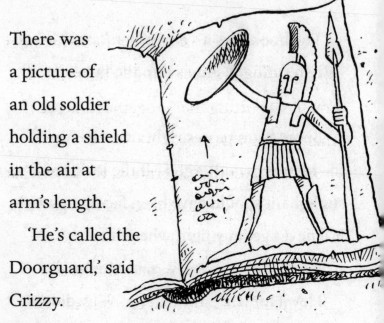

'He's called the
Doorguard,' said
Grizzy.

'He was twice the size of a normal
person,' said Hunjah proudly.

'If he's supposed to be guarding a door,
he's useless,' said Borgon. 'Why is he holding
his shield up like that?'

'It's another mystery!' said Mungoid.

'I've got an idea,' said Borgon. 'Remember all those bits of statue lying in the sand? We could try putting them together and see if that tells us anything.'

And so later that afternoon, they were back by the temple door, digging around in the sand.

'Here's the flat bit of stone that the Doorguard used to stand on,' said Hunjah.

'It's a long way back from the door,' said Grizzy.

HISSSSSS!

Just then the blue snake came darting across towards them. The other three dashed off but Borgon went to stand in its way.

'Hello, mate!' said the axeboy. 'What do you want? Ready to be turned into bootlaces?'

The snake stopped and eyed Borgon warily.

Rattle rattle rattle! went its tail.

'Oh, behave!' said Borgon. 'I don't really want to turn you into bootlaces! I'll just call you Bootlace, how about that? Now keep out of the way and you'll be fine.'

The snake slithered past Borgon, then hurried over to wrap itself round a devil's thorn plant.

'Be careful, Bootlace!' said Borgon. 'Those thorns are nasty.'

The snake wrapped itself even tighter and

stared back at the axeboy crossly.

'Please yourself!' laughed Borgon, then he called out to the others. 'Come on, you lot. He only wants to watch us.'

They dug up all the pieces of the statue that they could find. The main body was

so heavy they couldn't even roll it. All they could do was drag the other bits over and put the stone soldier together, lying on his back.

Grizzy checked the picture in her book. 'He's just about all there,' she said. 'Apart from one thing.'

'His shield!' they all said.

Rattle rattle rattle!

The snake was twitching angrily.

'I bet I know where that shield is!' said Borgon. 'Do you mind if I look under your plant, Bootlace?'

The snake hissed at him.

'Hey, Borgon,' said Grizzy nervously.

'You're called the Axeboy. I wish you'd just chop that snake up!'

'I couldn't,' said Borgon. 'Can't you see? He's doing his best to guard something. He's a good lad, doing a good job.'

He grabbed the snake by the neck and tried to unwrap it from the plant, but the snake refused to let go. Finally Borgon pulled on the snake as hard as he could. The whole plant popped out of the ground, and down at the bottom of the hole, something glinted in the light.

'Found it!' said Borgon.

The snake gave up the struggle. Borgon carried the beast over to a rock by the temple wall and gently laid it out. The blue skin was peppered with devil's thorns, so Borgon carefully started pulling them out.

'This lot must really sting,' said Borgon to the snake. 'Why were you so desperate to stop us getting that shield?'

Mungoid held the shield up. It was like a shiny silver dinner plate with a handle on the back.

'This shield doesn't make sense!' said Mungoid.

'It's an odd shape and too heavy for fighting.'

'The statue was holding it in the air,' said Grizzy.

'You mean like this?' asked Mungoid.

He went to stand on the flat stone then held up the shield.

'**YOWWWWW!**' screamed Borgon.

The chubby little savage was hopping about clutching the seat of his trousers with smoke pouring out between his

fingers.

'His bottom's on fire!' said Mungoid.

'How did that happen?' asked Hunjah.

'Who cares?' laughed Grizzy. 'I hope it happens again.'

'Look!' said Hunjah.

A blinding white dot of light was flickering on the temple wall where Borgon had been standing. Hunjah put his hand in it.

'Ow!' he said, quickly pulling his hand back again. 'That's hot! It's sunlight, and it's shining off the shield.'

By this time, Borgon had cooled down and was getting his breath back. 'That's not a shield,' he groaned. 'It's a weapon!'

'You're both wrong,' said Grizzy.

'It's not a shield or a weapon. It's the key to the temple! Hey, Mungoid, try aiming the light at the sun lock.'

Mungoid tipped the shield so the white dot slid up the wall.

'I'm not as tall as the statue,' said Mungoid. 'I can't get it to shine right into the hole.'

Grizzy pointed over to a pile of big rocks glowing in the sunlight.

'Go and climb up there,' she said. 'Then see if you can do it.'

Mungoid scrambled up with the shield while Grizzy studied her book again.

'You need to be in exactly the right place,'

said Grizzy. 'Move along a bit, and then just a little bit higher . . .'

The white dot wiggled and wobbled over the temple wall, then settled in place on the little hole.

'That's it, Mungoid,' shouted Grizzy. 'Hold it steady.'

'It doesn't look as bright,' said Hunjah.

'That's because it's getting late,' said Borgon, looking up at the sky. 'The sun is going down.'

Just then the snake appeared, crawling along the top of the arch. It reached the little hole, then tucked itself in.

'It's blocked the lock!' said Borgon. 'That

snake does NOT want us to do this.'

'But surely it knows how hot that ray of sunlight can be,' said Grizzy. 'That snake will get burnt to bits.'

They all waited for the smell of burning snake, but it didn't happen.

'It's already too dark,' said Mungoid.

'It looks like the snake has won after all,' chuckled Borgon.

'No it has not!' said Grizzy crossly.

She snatched up a stone and threw it at the sun lock. The stone shot into the hole, and the snake tumbled out with an angry hiss.

'Too late,' said Borgon. 'The light's almost gone.'

'I told you it wouldn't work,' said Hunjah.
But then . . .

CREEEE–AKKKK!

A deep heavy rumble came from inside
the temple, and the great slab of stone
twitched . . . just a tiny bit.

'YES!' shouted Grizzy. 'YES YES YES! I
did it! I'm so CLEVER! Go on, Borgon, you
have to admit it. Say I'm clever!'

Borgon sighed. Of course Grizzy was clever,
but she could also be incredibly irritating.

'Why have I got to say you're clever?'
asked Borgon.

'Oh, come on!' said Grizzy, tugging his
sleeve. 'I made the door move.'

'Yes, but it didn't exactly fly wide open did it?' said Borgon.

'That's because the sun's gone down,' said Grizzy. 'But you still have to say I'm clever.'

'No I don't,' said Borgon. 'The sun always goes down. If you were clever, you would have thought of that.'

'Ha ha ha!' laughed the boys.

'Come on,' said Borgon. 'It's not worth staying out here in the dark. Maybe we'll come back and try it again tomorrow.'

And so it was that the four of them set off home with the three boys still giggling like tickled chimps, and Grizzy sulking like a wet cat.

Hunting Peaches

Next morning, as the sun rose above the
Lost Desert, there were strange noises
coming from the barbarians' cave.

KRONCH! KRUMP! KRAKK!

Borgon and Fulma were munching their
way through a giant basket of peaches.

'You're right, Mum,' said Borgon.

'The squishy bit is horrible but the middle bits are YUM!'

'Eat up,' said Fulma. 'There's lots more. I had no idea that little coin would be worth so much.'

Fulgut was sitting at the end of the cave being grumpy.

'Come on, Dad,' said Borgon. 'They're really nice.'

'I'm having nothing to do with them,' said Fulgut. 'Barbarians should HUNT their food, not buy it. Money just brings trouble.'

Then they heard voices coming from outside.

A grand sedan chair had pulled up near

their cave. It was being carried by two
big slaves, both armed with a long curved
sword. Hunjah was talking to a tall thin

man sitting on the seat. The man had a shiny head and long white robes and had huge gold rings dangling from his ears. He held out something small in his hand. Hunjah nodded, then pointed over to the barbarian's cave.

The man got down from the sedan chair and came over.

'What did I tell you?' growled Fulgut. 'Here comes somebody sticking his nose in.'

'I'll get rid of him,' said Borgon.

'I bet you can't,' said Fulgut. 'Not if he's heard about the money. You'd better leave it to your mum. After all, she is the scariest savage in the Lost Desert.'

'Not just now I'm not,' said Fulma, sticking her finger in her mouth. 'I've got a bit of peach skin stuck in my teeth.'

'Oh, go on then, Borgon,' said Fulgut. 'Do your best! But remember, do NOT tell him about the money.'

Borgon stepped out of the cave holding his axe and pulling his scary face.

'**GRRRR!**' he growled. 'We don't like visitors.'

That was usually enough to send strangers away, but the man just put on a big smile.

'Greetings!' he said. 'Your friend said you can help me.'

'Oh, he did, did he?' said Borgon, then he added an extra **GRRRR!**

The tall man held out the gold coin.

'I'm looking for the lady who spent this coin at the market,' said the man. 'A tall lady with dark red spiky hair.'

'I've no idea who she is,' said Borgon. 'Goodbye.'

But then the cave echoed with some **KRUNCH SLURP BURP!** noises. The man peered over Borgon's shoulder.

'But that lady in the cave is tall with dark red spiky hair,' said the man, with an even bigger smile.

'No she isn't,' said Borgon, feeling a bit silly.

'Are you sure?' asked the man. 'The lady was seen buying a huge basket of peaches.'

'We never buy peaches,' said Borgon.

SHPLIP! A soggy lump of peach flew out and landed at the man's feet.

The man was getting even smilier and Borgon felt even sillier.

'So tell me, how did that tall lady with dark red spiky hair get those peaches?' asked the tall man.

'We're BARBARIANS!' said Borgon getting desperate. 'We don't buy food. We HUNT food.'

Borgon gave his axe a wave and added an extra loud **GRRRR!** to make himself feel better.

'So you hunted a basket of peaches?' asked the man.

'Er . . . YES!' said Borgon. He was feeling like a real idiot. 'There was a giant peach tree charging across the desert, so we attacked it with swords and axes and chopped all its peaches off.'

'Oh,' said the man. 'That's a pity . . .'

He was twiddling the coin in front of Borgon's face.

'. . . because I actually came here to give the coin back.'

'Give it back?'

'Yes,' said the man. 'But if you've never seen it before, obviously I've got the wrong people.'

'Not so fast,' said Borgon. 'Why are you giving it back?'

'My name is Zaffar, and I look for lost temples,' said the man. 'This is an old temple coin, and I'll give it to the person who can tell me where it came from.'

'What do you want to know that for?' said Borgon.

'Ah! Er . . .' Zaffar looked confused. 'Um . . . Oh yes, I know! There's been a lot of trouble with some of the old desert gods. When they get forgotten, they get angry. They send plagues of frogs or leave quicksand traps and so on. It's my job to restore their temples to keep the gods happy.'

By this time, his smile was as big as a banana, but then Fulgut stepped out of the cave.

'Hey, Borgon, haven't you got rid of him yet?'

'He won't go,' said Borgon. 'He's looking for a tall lady with dark red spiky hair and a big basket of peaches.'

'Is he really?' said Fulgut. 'Does she look anything like this?'

Fulgut moved aside to reveal Fulma. She was pulling her scariest face. Her hair was sticking out like the spikes on a porcupine, her eyes were dark narrow slits, and her teeth glinted like a row of white needles.

'**ARGHHH!**' screamed the man, and he

ran all the way back to his sedan chair.

'That's got rid of him!' laughed Borgon. 'Well done, Mum!'

Then Borgon saw a straw hat twitching behind a rock.

'Hunjah!' said Borgon. 'Were you spying on us?'

'I was trying to,' said Hunjah. 'What did that man want?'

'He was asking where the temple was,' said Borgon. 'But don't worry, I didn't tell him.'

'Thank goodness,' said Hunjah. 'But why would he want to know?'

'No special reason,' said Borgon. 'He

just wants to build it up and make it nice again to keep the god happy . . . Hunjah? HUNJAH?'

But the skinny savage was already running off after the sedan chair as fast as he could.

'WAIT! STOP!' shouted Hunjah. 'I've got something to tell you!'

85

The Spank of Fire

Later that day, Borgon was back on top of
the temple ruins looking out for the two
slaves carrying the sedan chair. As soon as
he saw them approaching, he scrambled
down to the ground where Mungoid,
Hunjah and Grizzy were waiting. Mungoid
was polishing the shield.

'They're coming!' said Borgon. 'Do you all know what you have to do?'

'We're pretending the Great Conk can open his own temple door,' said Mungoid.

'Well I'm not helping you,' said Grizzy. 'Not after you all laughed at me yesterday.'

'Oh, come on, Grizzy,' said Borgon. 'Here's your chance! If you can really make this work, then we'll have to admit you're clever, won't we?'

Mungoid and Hunjah nodded.

'Very well,' said Grizzy. 'But I still can't see why we're bothering.'

'We want to make Zaffar think that this Conk god is big and powerful,' said Borgon.

'Then he might restore the temple and make it nice again.'

'What's the point?' said Grizzy. 'There is no Great Conk.'

'Yes there is,' said Hunjah. 'He made it rain and you saw his blue snake!'

'That was pathetic,' said Grizzy. 'If this Conk really was great, he'd make volcanoes explode and drop crocodiles on us or something good like that.'

'Don't be mean, Grizzy,' said Borgon. 'This old temple means a lot to Hunjah. All you've got to do is tell Mungoid where to hold the shield, so that the door opens.'

'Oh, all right,' said Grizzy. 'But don't

expect me to tell anybody there's a god in there, because there isn't.'

Mungoid and Grizzy went off to hide in the rocks.

'Are you sure the door will open?' asked Hunjah.

'It should do,' said Borgon. 'It would have opened last time if the sun hadn't gone down.'

'Oh,' said Hunjah. He sounded a bit gloomy.

'What's the matter?' asked Borgon.

'Nothing,' said Hunjah. 'It's just that when I was small, I really DID think the Great Conk opened the temple door. It turns out it was just a statue with a shiny shield all the time.'

'Never mind!' said Borgon. 'With our help, your god will get a grand new temple, and then maybe miracles *will* happen!'

The sedan chair came round the corner. Hunjah ran over to meet it.

'Welcome to the temple of the Great Conk,' he said excitedly.

'Where is it, my friend?' smiled the tall man.

'Here!' said Hunjah, pointing at the doorway. 'Inside there's a great big nose.'

The two big slaves carrying the sedan chair had a little giggle, which made the chair wobble. Zaffar's smile quickly turned to an angry scowl.

'Are you joking?' he said crossly. 'You've asked me to come all this way for a *big nose*?'

'Absolutely, and it's dripping!' said Hunjah. 'Are you ready to see it?'

'No I am not! You told me that this was the temple of a powerful god.'

'It is!' said Hunjah. 'Isn't it, Borgon?'

'Oh yes,' said Borgon. 'This temple belongs to the Great Conk, and he's not to be sniffed at.'

Zaffar took a closer look at the little

chubby savage. 'Oh, it's you!' he said. 'You're the boy who makes up stories about fighting peach trees.'

'**GRRRR!**' growled Borgon. The tall man with the shiny head was making him feel silly again. In fact there was something about this man that he didn't like, but Borgon knew he had to be nice, or he'd ruin Hunjah's chances of getting the temple fixed up.

'Is there anything else in there apart from a nose?' asked Zaffar. 'Some gold statues perhaps? Or maybe the floor is covered in precious stones?'

'I don't think so,' said Hunjah. 'All I can

remember is the nose. Oh, and the offerings of course.'

'Offerings?' said Zaffar. 'You mean presents to the god?'

'That's right,' said Hunjah. 'There's a huge pile of them.'

Zaffar pulled the gold coin out of his pocket. 'You mean like this?'

'That's just one little coin,' said Hunjah. 'People used to bring loads of stuff to make the Great Conk happy.'

'Loads of stuff?' repeated Zaffar. The smile came back to his face.

'Oh yes,' said Hunjah. 'In fact, if you see anything you like, you can have it.'

'Hunjah!' said Borgon. 'You can't just let him take whatever he wants!'

'Why not?' said Hunjah. 'The Great Conk won't mind.'

'Really?' said Zaffar.

'Of course,' said Hunjah. 'Just so long as you restore the temple, like you said you would.'

'Restore the temple?' said Zaffar, looking puzzled. 'Did I say that?'

'Yes you did!' growled Borgon crossly. He really didn't like this thin man at all.

'Oh yes, that's right. I remember now,' said Zaffar, then he turned to his slaves. 'We'll restore the temple, won't we, boys?'

'Restore it?' said the big slaves. 'But we thought we were just here to . . .'

'Shhh!' said Zaffar. 'No time for chatter. Bring your hammers, we'll soon smash through this door.'

Zaffar leapt down from his sedan chair and the slaves pulled out some huge metal mallets.

'Sorry!' said Hunjah. 'You can't do that. You have to ask the Great Conk to open the door.'

'Don't be silly,' said Zaffar. 'Get to it, boys.'

The slaves stepped forwards, but then something dropped from the top of the archway and landed in front of them. It was

the blue snake! It raised its head and hissed
angrily.

Rattle rattle rattle!

The slaves leapt backwards, then tried to
swipe at the snake with their mallets. The
snake dodged them easily.

PTHHRB!

'Ha ha! You two are useless!' laughed Borgon. 'Come here, Bootlace!'

He pushed past the slaves, but the snake saw him coming. It was obviously bored of being grabbed, so instead it dashed off round the corner.

'Thank you,' said Zaffar. 'Now stand aside so we can break in.'

But Borgon stayed where he was. He'd spotted Mungoid and Grizzy up in the rocks waving at him. Mungoid was pointing at the shield and Grizzy was pointing at Zaffar. Borgon grinned. He knew exactly what they were thinking!

'Don't try to break in,' warned Borgon.

'Or the Great Conk will spank you
with his hand of fire!'

'I don't believe you and your silly stories,'
said Zaffar.

'Don't you?' said Borgon. He looked
upwards and called out in a big voice.
'Oh, Great Conk! Let the
unbeliever feel your power!'

Borgon saw the sunlight
glint off the shield.

'Oh really,' said
Zaffar. 'We haven't
got time for this . . .
YAROOOOP!'

The tall man hopped

and jumped around with smoke coming up from his bottom. Mungoid and Grizzy ducked down behind the rocks to avoid being spotted.

'Let that be a lesson to you!' said Borgon. 'If you want to get inside, do as Hunjah says.'

'You have to bow down low,' said Hunjah. 'Then shout out, *Oh, Great Conk, open the door, I beg you!*'

Zaffar was trembling and the two slaves were watching nervously.

'Or maybe that big pile of offerings isn't any use to you?' said Borgon.

Zaffar slowly got to his knees.

Borgon glanced up at the rocks to see

if Mungoid and Grizzy were ready, but
Mungoid had his hands clamped over his
mouth, desperately trying not to laugh.
Grizzy pointed at Hunjah, then she pointed
at her foot and puckered her lips.

'Oh, sorry!' said Borgon. 'There's just one
more thing.'

'What?' asked Zaffar.

Borgon pushed Hunjah forwards.

'This guy's mum was a priestess here,' said
Borgon. 'So after you've shouted, you have
to kiss his feet.'

'He doesn't have to do that!' said Hunjah.

'I think he should,' said Borgon. 'Just to be
on the safe side.'

'Never!' said Zaffar.

'Think of that big pile of offerings,' said Borgon.

Zaffar growled crossly, but then shouted:

'Oh, Great Conk, open the door, I beg you!'

And he kissed Hunjah's feet.

The shield glinted from the rocks again. The light flickered around the sun lock, and then from inside the temple came a low

CREAKKKK!

'Oooh . . .' said Zaffar.

CREAKKKK!

'OOOH!' said the slaves.

KUR-RARRK!

The stone door twitched. A few dried-out mushrooms fell away from the cracks.

RUMBLE SHUDDER!

The door slowly crept upwards. A stink of mouldy dampness wafted towards them.

'It's opening!' yelped Hunjah in delight.

They all watched in amazement as the stone slab went up and disappeared into the top of the arch. Inside it was pitch black.

'I don't believe it!' gasped Zaffar.

'You know what the Great Conk does to unbelievers,' said Borgon.

'Sorry!' said Zaffar. 'SORRY!' he shouted into the temple.

The Hungry God

Zaffar and his slaves had gathered round the temple door. They had lit some burning torches and were peering into the darkness. While their backs were turned, Grizzy slipped down from the rocks and came running over to Borgon.

'It worked!' she whispered excitedly.

'So you have to tell me how clever I am.'

'You're very clever,' admitted Borgon. 'Does Mungoid know what he's doing with that shield?'

'He's fine,' said Grizzy. 'As long as he keeps the light on the sun lock, the door should stay open.'

'Where did she come from?' asked Zaffar, seeing Grizzy.

'I just fell out of the sky,' said Grizzy. 'Why, what's it to you?'

'He's a bit worried,' said Borgon. 'The Great Conk just gave him a spank of fire.'

'Oh, how very awful,' said Grizzy.

'So are you going inside then?' Hunjah

asked Zaffar.

'He's got to pay you first,' said Borgon. 'He said he'd give you that gold coin for telling him where the temple is.'

'You'll get the coin once I've been inside and seen it for myself,' said Zaffar. 'But you three have to go in first.'

'What's your problem?' asked Borgon.

'I don't trust this god of yours,' said Zaffar. 'There might be traps.'

'Let me go first then!' said Hunjah. 'I'll be safe. The Great Conk likes me.'

The weedy savage stepped into the darkness, then from outside they heard his voice.

'Oh, mighty me! Hey, Borgon, Grizzy, get in here!'

Borgon went in, followed by Grizzy close behind. As they got used to the light, they saw two large empty eyeholes high on the far wall, and the giant nose sticking out between them. On the floor underneath was a massive stinking pile of something. Water was dribbling down the side of it.

PLIP PLOP PLUB!

'That nose is still dripping!' said Grizzy.

'I know,' said Hunjah. 'And we were standing up there inside yesterday. Isn't it fantastic?'

The rest of the god was carved around the temple wall. He was lying on his side with his head propped up and wearing massive baggy trousers. Although his nose was by far his biggest feature, his naked belly was sticking out as large and as round as an elephant's bottom.

'Listen!' said Borgon. 'Can you two hear a noise?'

There was a soft buzz echoing around the temple. It was like an army of people

all whispering at once. Borgon put his ear
to the god's belly button. There was a little
dark hole and the noise was coming from
deep inside, but he couldn't make out any
words. It was a bit creepy. Oo-er!

'What's making that noise?' asked Borgon.

'I don't know,' said Hunjah. 'Maybe we'll
find out when the temple gets restored.'

'What's going on in there?' came Zaffar's

111

voice from the doorway. 'Are you lot still alive?'

'No, I'm a ghost,' shouted Grizzy. 'Wooo!'

'Ignore her!' shouted Hunjah. 'Come on in.'

Zaffar and the slaves stepped inside. They stuck their burning torches into holders on the wall then peered around in the gloom.

'It's disgusting!' said Zaffar, wrinkling his nose.

'Mind your manners,' said Borgon. 'The Great Conk might hear you.'

'Really?' said Zaffar, then he cried out: 'Listen here, Great Conk! Here's the deal. You let us take some of your offerings, and

112

then we'll restore your temple. How about that?'

Nothing happened.

'Well, he's not complaining,' said Zaffar. 'So where is this great pile of offerings?'

'Underneath the nose,' said Hunjah.

Zaffar went over to the stinking pile. He stuck his hand into it, then quickly pulled it back.

'What IS this?' he demanded, looking at his fingers.

'The offerings,' said Hunjah. 'Do help yourself.'

'I thought it was going to be a pile of treasure,' said Zaffar.

'Oh no!' said Hunjah. 'Maybe there were one or two coins, but that's not what the Great Conk likes.'

'So what is it?'

'Sandwiches mainly,' said Hunjah.

'SANDWICHES?' repeated Zaffar.

'Ha ha ha!' laughed Grizzy.

'What's so funny?' said Hunjah, sounding a bit peeved. 'The Great Conk likes tomatoes too. And pies and pickled onions and boiled eggs.'

'But it's all slimy!' said Zaffar.

'That pile has been there for many years,' said Hunjah. 'With the nose dripping on it.'

Borgon was amazed. Was it possible that Hunjah's god was even more pathetic than Hunjah was?

'Tell us, Hunjah,' said Borgon. 'Exactly what kind of god is the Great Conk?'

'He's a nice god,' said Hunjah.

'We know that,' said Borgon. 'But is he a war god? Or a river god, or one of the fire gods?'

'Didn't I say?' said Hunjah. 'The Great Conk is the god of picnics.'

'PICNICS?' they all gasped.

'That's right,' said Hunjah. 'If people were going on a picnic, they would offer the Great Conk a sandwich or something to make sure the weather stayed nice. But if anyone upset the Great Conk, he would send showers of rain out of his nose.'

'Are you serious?' asked Zaffar.

'Of course,' said Hunjah. 'That's what he does. The Wrath of Conk is mighty.'

Borgon felt so sorry for Hunjah. His god WAS even more pathetic than he was.

'And was your mother really a priestess for this odd little god?' asked Zaffar.

'Yes,' said Hunjah proudly. 'She used to pour out the orange juice. She even helped with a barbecue once. She loved it.'

'Then she is an idiot!' cursed Zaffar.

'No she is NOT,' said Hunjah. 'So are you going to restore the temple?'

'My dear child,' said Zaffar. 'We only came here to see if there was anything worth taking. Do you really believe that we go round the desert restoring disgusting little temples? You must be as daft as your mother.'

Zaffar and the slaves all laughed. Hunjah tried to look brave, but then he burst into tears and ran out of the temple.

'Come on, men, there's nothing for us in here, let's go,' said Zaffar and they turned away.

But Borgon was standing in the doorway, and he was holding his axe. He'd been waiting for an excuse for a fight, and now he'd got one!

'You're going nowhere,' said the young barbarian. 'You've upset my mate, and

118

what's more, you made a deal.'

'What deal?'

'He showed you the temple, so you hand over that coin.'

Zaffar pulled the coin from his robes. The two slaves gathered in front of him with their swords drawn.

'You want it?' said Zaffar with a wicked grin. 'Then you come and get it.'

'Thanks!' said Borgon. 'I thought you'd never ask. **YARGHHHHH!**'

Mushroom and Cucumber Sandwiches

Borgon attacked so fast the slaves hardly saw him coming. He slipped his axe handle between one slave's feet. The man spun round and dived head first into the heap of offerings.

SPLOMPCH!

A cloud of stink wafted across the temple. The top half of the slave was completely buried, with just his legs sticking out. He kicked and twisted to pull himself free, and slowly it all started to topple over.

A cascade of squelchy sandwiches came tumbling down, manky pies rolled along the floor and a shower of hard-boiled eggs bounced off the walls. The slave coughed and spluttered and staggered around scraping the mouldy slime from his face.

'That is GROSS!' exclaimed Grizzy, who had been keeping well out of the way.

'Lovely, isn't it?' laughed Borgon, as the other slave's sword flashed towards him.

With a flick of his axe, Borgon sent the blade spinning away through the air. The slave slipped on a bunch of gassy grapes and skidded **WEEE-BOILCH!** straight into a sack of sloppy old tomatoes. Zaffar was furious.

'Come on, you clowns!' snapped the tall man angrily. 'He's only a boy! Get him!'

The slaves picked up their swords, then they both charged together, but Borgon threw himself to the ground and whacked their knees with the back of his axe.

'YOW!' they yelped and somersaulted backwards into a slimy pile of old mushroom and cucumber sandwiches.

PLUMPCH!

Borgon jumped to his feet. The defeated slaves had crawled off into a corner but Zaffar was aiming a crossbow right at his chest.

'You're very good with your axe,' said Zaffar. 'But the arrow on this crossbow is dipped in red-toad poison and I never miss. You've tried to make me look foolish, Axeboy. That was a mistake. Goodbye.'

Zaffar raised the crossbow to fire, but over

in the far darkness of the temple, Grizzy had
grabbed something from the ground and
threw it.

SPLOOF!

A two-hundred-
year-old pickled
onion hit Zaffar
right in the face.

'Good one,
Grizzy!' said Borgon.

**'Gugg-gugg-
guggah!'** choked Zaffar,
as the stinging fumes

shot up his
nose. He rolled
over, wiping his eyes
and gasping for air.

PER-TWANG!

The tiny arrow shot off across the
temple and then . . .

THUNG!

'What was that noise?' asked Grizzy.

She went over and saw a large black
curtain hanging down. She pulled it aside.

'Oh wow!' said Grizzy. 'Look at this,
Borgon.'

Hanging from a thick wooden frame
was a bell. It shone in the darkness with a

125

strange yellow glow.
Sitting on the top with
its head raised and his
fangs bared was the
blue snake.

Rattle rattle rattle!

'Hello, Bootlace!' said Borgon. 'I
wondered where you'd got to!'

He gave the bell a little tap.

THUNG!

'Nice noise!' said Grizzy. 'The arrow must
have shot through the curtain and hit it. But
what's it made of?'

'It's gold, you fools!' said Zaffar from

across the room. 'It's a calling bell to summon the gods.'

'So this is what Bootlace has been guarding all the time,' said Borgon.

'That's changed the situation!' said the tall man. 'You can have your coin after all, if you get rid of the snake and we can take the bell.'

'No way!' said Borgon. 'This bell belongs to Hunjah's god. It stays here.'

'Your friend said I could take what I wanted,' said Zaffar.

'That's when he thought you were going to rebuild his temple,' said Borgon. 'So keep your little coin and go.'

Borgon had his axe raised and was forcing

Zaffar and the two slaves back towards the doorway.

'You can't win,' said Zaffar. 'You can't guard this place all the time. We'll be back for that bell.'

'What if the door's closed?' said Grizzy.

'We can smash it down,' said Zaffar.

'The god won't let you!' said Borgon. 'Don't forget how he burnt you on the bottom last time! Isn't that right, Grizzy?'

'Humf!' said Grizzy, shaking her head crossly.

'Humf?' said Zaffar suspiciously. 'Surely it must have been a god . . . unless it was a very clever trick.'

'Very clever!' agreed Grizzy excitedly. 'And making the temple door open would be clever too, wouldn't you say?'

'Grizzy!' said Borgon. 'Be quiet!'

'It would be very clever indeed,' said Zaffar sounding surprised. 'But no human could have done it.'

'That's where you're wrong!' said Grizzy, looking very pleased with herself. 'The door opens with a sun lock.'

'A sun lock?' repeated Zaffar.

Grizzy waved her book.

'It's all in here!' she said. 'There's a hole in the wall with an old strip of leather hanging inside. When the sunlight heats the leather up, it shrinks and pulls a little lever. Then a big heavy weight falls down on a rope and that pulls the door up. See? It was ME all the time!'

'So you mean there's no god here after all?' said Zaffar.

'Of course there's no god!' said Grizzy. 'I'll prove it to you.'

Before Borgon could stop her, she ran over to the bell and banged it as loudly as she could.

DONG DANG DUNG . . .

'HEY, GREAT CONK, THIS IS YOUR LAST CHANCE!' she shouted. 'SHOW YOURSELF!'

The sounds of the bell slowly echoed and died away.

'See?' said Grizzy. 'It was me.'

'NO!' came a huge voice that boomed all around the temple. 'IT WAS ME!'

The Wrath of Conk

Everything in the temple rattled. Loose
stones tumbled from the roof, boiled eggs
bounced along the floor, and the whispering
noise in the walls suddenly got much louder.

Borgon, Grizzy, Zaffar and his men, and
even the blue snake all stared up at the big
nose in astonishment.

'What . . . what was that?' whispered Grizzy. Her voice was trembling.

'You've summoned the Great Conk!' gasped Borgon.

'SILENCE!' said the voice. 'FALL TO YOUR FACES BEFORE ME . . . OR FEEL THE WRATH OF CONK!'

They all threw themselves to the ground and lay there face down.

'WHO LIES BEFORE ME?'

'It is I, your servant, Borgon!' said Borgon.

'And I, your even bigger servant, Grizzy,' said Grizzy.

'AND WHO HAS COME TO STEAL FROM MY HOUSE?' cried the voice.

'Not me!' squealed Grizzy. 'Please, let me go! I'll worship you forever.'

'SILENCE,' said the voice. 'FOR I KNOW WHO THE THIEF IS!'

Zaffar was shaking.

'What? Me? Oh no. You've got it wrong!' he said. 'I came to rebuild your temple.'

'YOU LIE!' boomed the voice. 'FOR I KNOW EVERYTHING. I SEE EVERYTHING. I SMELL EVERYTHING . . . OH NO, I DROPPED MY HAT AGAIN.'

'What?' said Zaffar suspiciously.

'NOTHING,' said the voice.

But then something fluttered down from

the great nose and landed on
the floor in front of Zaffar.

A thin arm came out
of the nose hole and was
feeling around.

'OH NO, MY MUM
WILL GO MAD!' said the
great voice.

Zaffar jumped up,
grabbed the arm and pulled
as hard as he could.
With a squeeze and a
plop, a weedy body
tumbled out of the
huge nose.

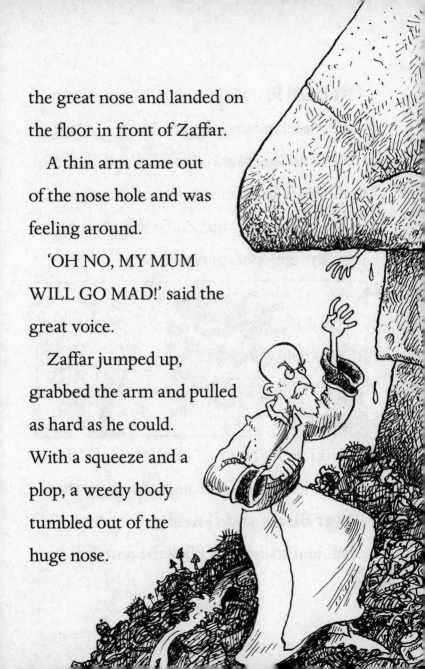

WHUMP!

Hunjah landed on top of Zaffar, but the tall man rolled him over and grabbed him by the neck. Borgon charged forwards to rescue the weedy savage, but Zaffar snatched up a mouldy hippopotamus pie.

'Stop there, Axeboy!' commanded Zaffar. He stuck his finger through the crust, then shoved the pie up to Hunjah's face. The smell of rotting meat filled the temple.

Hunjah had his mouth clamped tight shut, and tears were streaming down his cheeks.

'All right, you two,' said Zaffar. 'Both of you, get back against the wall. Let my men take that bell or your friend starts eating his last ever meal.'

'I DON'T CARE,' shouted Grizzy crossly. 'I HATE him.'

'Just do it, Grizzy,' said Borgon. 'Hunjah's in big danger here. This is no time to be clever.'

'I'm not standing by any wall to save Hunjah,' said Grizzy. 'Honestly, Hunjah, I can't believe you made me fall flat on my face. I feel such an idiot. I'll NEVER forgive you for this.'

'But I was protecting the Great Conk's temple,' gasped Hunjah, then he quickly clamped his mouth shut again.

'For the last time, there is no Great Conk!' said Grizzy. 'This is just a big smelly room with a pile of mouldy sandwiches.'

'The girl is right,' said Zaffar. 'So you two get out of the way, and let my men out with the bell.'

'NO!' shouted Hunjah. He struggled to get free but Zaffar pushed the pie closer to his face.

'If you hurt him . . .' warned Borgon, waving his axe.

'Throw that axe away NOW, or your

friend gets it,' said Zaffar.

'No, Borgon!' cried Hunjah. 'You've got to save the bell! It doesn't matter what happens to me.'

'**GRRRR!**' growled Borgon. He was desperate to attack, but he couldn't bear to think what that stinky hippopotamus pie might do to Hunjah. Maybe Hunjah was pathetic, but he was also one of the bravest savages that had ever lived.

'Sorry, Hunjah,' said Borgon. He threw his axe away across the room where it landed on a cheese and dungbeetle flan.

BOILCH!

The two slaves went to get the bell but the blue snake was still guarding it.

Rattle rattle rattle!

'You've done your job well, Bootlace,' said Borgon. 'But we have to let them take it.'

The snake hissed and all around them the whispering noise got louder again.

Suddenly a chunky figure charged in from outside.

'Quick!' shouted Mungoid. 'All of you, get out! The door is going to close.'

'Who's he?' demanded Zaffar.

'He's supposed to be keeping the light on the sun lock,' said Grizzy.

'I can't,' said Mungoid. 'There's a cloud blocking the sun.'

'It'll soon pass,' said Zaffar.

'It won't!' said Mungoid. 'It's just sitting there . . . and guess what shape it is?'

'It's a big nose!' cheered Hunjah.

RUMBLE RUMBLE!

The stone slab was slowly coming down from the top of the archway. The slaves ran towards the door, but Zaffar didn't budge.

'Get back here, you two!' he ordered. 'We're not going without that bell.'

'Well, I am!' said Grizzy. 'Borgon, come on.'

'I'm not leaving Hunjah to face that dangerous pie on his own,' said Borgon.

'If Borgon's staying, then I'm staying,' said Mungoid.

'You're all mad!' said Grizzy. 'We could be stuck in here forever!'

RUMBLE RUMBLE!

The door had come down as far as shoulder height.

'Let's go!' shouted Grizzy, then she ducked underneath and ran out.

RUMBLE RUMBLE RUMBLE!

The door had got to knee height when suddenly Grizzy's head and shoulders

appeared back underneath. She scrabbled herself forwards on her elbows, and just pulled her feet through as the stone hit the ground with a soft

THUDDD!

Grizzy stood up, flicked the sand out of her hair and stared at them crossly.

'You lot are SO selfish,' said Grizzy. 'I can't believe you'd make me wait outside there all on my own.'

'So what happens now?' asked Mungoid. 'Are we really stuck here forever?'

'No,' said Zaffar. He clicked his fingers. The two slaves picked up their swords and faced the three young savages.

'The girl will have to climb out of the nose and get the door open again,' said Zaffar.

'Not me!' said Grizzy. 'I'm not going up a drippy nose. No way.'

'It has to be you,' said Zaffar. 'You're the only one slim enough and clever enough.'

Grizzy hissed crossly. 'And what makes you think I won't just run off and leave you all?'

'Because you came back when the door was closing,' said Zaffar. 'You might pretend that you don't care about the boys, but you do.'

Grizzy stamped her feet angrily.

144

'I wish I wasn't so NICE,' she shouted. 'Borgon, Mungoid, come here and give me a lift up.'

Mungoid stood underneath the nose, then Borgon climbed on to his shoulders. Grizzy climbed all the way up them both then reached up into the hole.

'Hey Mungoid,' said Borgon. 'I never thought we'd get the chance to shove Grizzy into a giant nose.'

'Ha ha ha!' laughed Mungoid.

'IT'S NOT FUNNY!' shouted Grizzy.

'Oh yes it is!' said Borgon. 'Ha ha ha!'

The boys started shaking so much that all three of them tumbled down.

The two slaves leapt forwards waving their swords angrily.

'If you want to live, get back up there NOW!' said Zaffar.

'No, don't,' said Hunjah. 'It's better that we all die!'

'Then we'll all die then,' said Grizzy. 'I'm not going up that big nose with those two laughing at me.'

'Then you give me NO CHOICE,' shouted Zaffar. 'Kill them! Kill them all!'

And that's when the whispering noise grew into a very loud and very angry BUZZZZZ.

The Deadly Whisper

The whole temple was echoing with the noise. Borgon ran to the statue's belly button and put his ear to the hole. The sound coming out was loud enough to make his eyes water.

'There's something alive in there,' said Borgon. 'Do you know what it is, Bootlace?'

He looked over at the bell, but the blue snake had gone. Borgon just saw the end of the rattlesnake's tail as it disappeared into a tiny crack in the floor.

'Whatever it is, Bootlace isn't waiting to see it!' said Mungoid.

Suddenly something small and buzzy popped out of the hole and hovered in the air. Borgon carefully closed his hand around it. He peered through his fingers, but when he saw the black and red stripes and the long pointed tail, he quickly let it go. More bugs were popping out, then more and more and even more.

'So that's what's making the noise!' said

Mungoid. 'What are they?'

'Fire wasps,' said Borgon. 'The ones with the sparking stings.'

'EEEEK!' shrieked Grizzy.

BZzZzzZZZzZzZ!

By this time the slaves had forgotten about the young savages. They were staring nervously at the swarm of bugs that was gathering in the middle of the temple.

'Well?' snapped Zaffar. 'What are you two waiting for? Get rid of them!'

The two slaves raised their swords, but the swarm went flying off round the temple like a runaway train.

BZzZzzZZZzZzZ!

The bugs darted
between Borgon and
Mungoid then went to
hover in a think cloud around
Grizzy's head. She dropped to
the floor and curled herself up into
a little ball.

'Help! No! Get them away!'
she cried.

But Grizzy wasn't
what the bugs were
looking for.
Suddenly they
all rose up and
headed towards

the slaves. The big men started slashing at the swarm with their swords, but that only made the bugs angrier. A few wasps landed on their shoulders, and then more and more came to join them, covering their necks and finally their heads. The slaves dropped their swords and tried to wipe the bugs away.

'Don't do that!' Borgon warned them. 'Stay very still! Once fire wasps have settled, they hate to be disturbed.'

Both men stood like statues, each of them covered in a thick black buzzing blanket of wasps.

'How come the wasps ignored us, and went for those two?' asked Mungoid.

'I don't know,' said Borgon. 'But look where the others are going!'

BZZzZzzzZZZZzZzZ!

The rest of the wasps had streamed across the temple towards Zaffar. The tall man shrieked in horror. He tried to hold Hunjah up as a shield, but it was useless.

'None of them are landing on Hunjah,' said Mungoid. 'They're all going for Zaffar!'

'It's as if they are being controlled by something,' said Borgon.

'Or some-*one*!' said Mungoid.

Zaffar threw Hunjah aside and ran screaming round

the temple, chased by the wasps.

BZZzZzzzZZZZzZzZ!

'Is your god doing this, Hunjah?' asked Mungoid.

'We thought he just dripped rain from his nose to spoil picnics,' said Borgon.

'It looks like he can shoot fire wasps from his belly button too,' said Hunjah proudly. 'And that would REALLY spoil a picnic! Nobody can call him pathetic now.'

By this time Zaffar was banging his fists on the temple door. The wasps were landing on his back, his head, his arms, his legs and every other part of his body.

'HELP! STOP THEM! LET ME

OUT!' he cried.

'First you must beg
the Great Conk for
mercy,' said Hunjah.

'NEVER!' shouted
Zaffar.

TZING!

A sizzling flash
of red light shot
from his neck.

'YOW!' screamed
Zaffar.

'That sounded
sore!' said Mungoid.

'And that was just

the first sting,' said Borgon. 'What happens if the others start stinging him too?'

'I can tell you that,' said Grizzy. She had got up and was reading her book excitedly. 'It says here that three fire wasp stings can make an elephant jump in the air. And five stings can blow the stripes off a zebra, and seven stings make you swell up and burst.'

'Hey, Zaffar,' said Borgon. 'I'd start begging for mercy if I was you.'

'NO!' said Zaffar but then there was another even bigger flash. 'YOW OW OOYAH! Please Great Conk, I beg of you! MERCY!'

But the door did not open.

'Maybe you have to promise not to come back,' said Hunjah.

'I promise,' whimpered Zaffar.

'Oh, and you have to say sorry to Borgon and Mungoid for bossing them around,' said Hunjah.

'Sorry sorry sorry!'

'And say that Grizzy is a very nice person and very clever too,' said Hunjah.

'Grizzy is a very nice person and very clever too,' said Zaffar.

The door was still shut.

'Oh dear, it's not working,' said Hunjah. 'And I can't think of anything else.'

'I can,' said Borgon. 'Tell Hunjah he's the

bravest person you've ever met.'

'Hunjah, you're the bravest!' said Zaffar.

'Really?' said Hunjah. 'Oh, thanks!'

RUMBLE . . . ZONK!

The stone door suddenly shot open.

Zaffar stumbled out followed by his

two slaves. Borgon, Hunjah, Mungoid and Grizzy followed them out into the daylight and watched as all three men ran away as fast and as far as they could.

'The Great Conk will never get his temple restored now,' said Hunjah sadly.

'Never mind,' said Borgon. 'Maybe he was the one who sent that little earthquake in the first place.'

'Why would he do that?' asked Mungoid.

'To stop people bothering him,' said Borgon. 'Maybe he's just old and tired and wants to be left alone.'

'Do you think so?' asked Hunjah. 'But how could we be sure?'

THUDDD!

The temple door dropped shut behind them.

Thank You, Bootlace!

That night Borgon could NOT get to sleep. He could hear Fulgut and Fulma happily snoring away in the back of the cave, but he was lying awake on his mammoth-skin rug in the entrance and staring up at the stars.

'Well, Great Conk, are you there or not?'

he asked. 'Because if you are, I'm very cross with you!'

It was the first night Borgon the Axeboy had ever gone to bed without his axe by his side. It was still locked in the temple, lying on the floor somewhere. Mungoid and Grizzy had tried to open the door again, but the sun lock had stopped working. Hunjah had offered to climb down from the big nose and see if he could find the axe, but it was a long drop and Bootlace was probably still in there doing his job.

'**GRRRR!**,' said Borgon. He felt so silly. What was the point of being Borgon the Axeboy without his axe? He'd just be Borgon the Boy, which was a pathetic name for a barbarian. The worst thing was that he'd lost his axe trying to protect the temple, when Borgon wasn't even sure if the Great Conk was real or not.

Of course Hunjah believed in the Great Conk. Mungoid said he believed too, but maybe he was just being nice to make Hunjah feel better.

Grizzy was the only one who refused to believe in the Great Conk. She had a simple way to explain everything that had happened.

What did she say when the rain first came down?

'It's just a funny-shaped cloud.'

What did she say when the wasps only attacked Zaffar and his men?

'They must smell of something that wasps like.'

What did she say when the temple door suddenly opened, then shut again?'

'That sun lock is so old it's gone faulty, and now it's completely broken.'

The more Borgon thought about it, the more he thought Grizzy was right.

'**GRRRR!**' said Borgon again.

He rolled over and squeezed his eyes shut, but they pinged open again. Strange little noises were coming from the other side of Golgarth Basin.

SCRITCH! HISS– A–PUFF!

SCRITCH! HISS– A–PUFF!

He peered out and saw something wriggling towards him in the darkness.

'It's Bootlace!' he said. 'What are you doing?'

The blue snake's head looked most peculiar. It wasn't until it got closer that Borgon realised he was looking at the rattlesnake's tail. The snake was moving backwards, and pulling something along with his mouth.

SCRITCH!

The snake did another move, then took a

deep breath . . .

HISS–A–PUFF!

'My axe!' said Borgon delightedly. 'You brought my axe back!'

He dashed over and picked up his trusty weapon. The snake lay there puffing away, getting its breath back.

'Have you really dragged it all the way from the temple?' asked Borgon. 'And how did you get it out? Did the door open? And how did you know where I live?'

The snake raised its head, but didn't bare its fangs. Borgon reached down and gave it a stroke. The snake gave a friendly little wave of its tail, then crept away into the darkness.

Borgon lay back down on his rug and this time his eyes dropped shut straight away.

'Thank you, Bootlace!' he said with a big happy yawn. He gave his axe a hug. 'I can't wait to see how Grizzy is going to explain this!'

And then, far across the desert, there was a soft rumble as the temple door closed for the very last time.